George Lansing Raymond

Colony Ballads

George Lansing Raymond

Colony Ballads

ISBN/EAN: 9783744784344

Printed in Europe, USA, Canada, Australia, Japan

Cover: Foto ©Andreas Hilbeck / pixelio.de

More available books at **www.hansebooks.com**

COLONY BALLADS

AN ATTEMPT TO REPRESENT SOMETHING OF THE SPIRIT
AND THE CIRCUMSTANCES ATTENDING THE SEP-
ARATION OF THE BRITISH COLONIES OF
MIDDLE NORTH AMERICA FROM
THEIR MOTHER COUNTRY

GEORGE L. RAYMOND

NEW YORK
PUBLISHED BY HURD AND HOUGHTON
Cambridge: The Riverside Press
1877

CONTENTS.

——◆——

COLONY BALLADS.

OUR FIRST BREAK WITH THE BRITISH.

1765.

GREAT BRITAIN'S lords in council,
　　As all things bore report,
Had planned, like royal liveries,
New modes to fit the colonies
　　To further serve the court.

If, brought to form one body,
　　The colonies now ally;
What comes, to pall their freedom all,
Will prove, so Franklin thought, too small.—
　　"We join," he wrote, "or die."

1

And "Freedom is a birthright
　　Our fathers hand us down;
Blood-bought," the lawyer Otis said:
" One king of old it cost his head;
　　And one his throne and crown.

" If lost in young New England,
　　Old England's, our mishap!
We lesser fish that flounder here
About the outer edges fear
　　But nets that all entrap.

" Our laws are in our charters
　　For scores of years enjoyed;
Nor court, nor king, nor mere consent
Of merely King and Parliament,
　　Has power to make them void.

" By these, and Magna Charta;
　　By all our Saxon rights;
By claims of nature, mind, descent;
A protest sent to Parliament
　　Should show what now it slights."

The people sent their protest,
  The lords, in naught restrained,
Tore the laws, to freedom's grief;
Each sail from England sped, a leaf
  To show that madness reigned.

Dissolved were our assemblies;
  Supreme the generals made;
Removed the judge our rights decreed;
And on the church our fathers freed
  The hands of bishops laid.

" Our Pilgrim race," preached Mayhew,
  " Were called to liberty;
And free, this side the deep, must be
Though madcaps, chasing, make the sea
  Blood-red with chivalry.

" The clouds about and waters
  Are His who guides the church;
And earth that heeds how Plymouth Rock,
To whelm the foe, throws back the shock,
  Shall yet our secret search."

"God guide the House of Commons!"
    We cried, with lifted eyes.
    God guided them and us, alas
    But all our Heaven He scorched to pass
      His finger through the skies.

    The Stamp Act came to test us.
      It laid the lash on each.
    To ship, to wed, to loan, to own,
    Were safe henceforth for him alone
      Whose seal belied his speech.

"Stamped papers bring but vouchers,"
    Wrote Green, "to license knaves."
"To tax us," Adams said nor bent,
"Where none our people represent
    Is but to brand us slaves.

"Our chartered free assemblies,
    The men we choose and arm
    With power to tax, and pay and stay
    The governor's, general's, judge's sway,
      Alone keep each from harm."

" Alone ! " cried Thomas Chase then,
   " But British agents curse
To find that our assemblies true
Find something nobler here to do
   Than fill a noble's purse."

" And therefore," Hancock added,
   " To plunder yet, prepare
This law that all their fleet empowers
To seize each honest ship of ours,
   And wrest a bounty there.

" Then, freely thus to plunder,
   They force our merchants wronged
Redress to seek in foreign courts
From him alone the gold supports
   That once to them belonged.

" For one my fleet shall carry
   No stamp though all I lose.
If England take, I hold my soul."
The people heard, and soon the whole
   Had vowed no stamps to use.

New York had lived by commerce.
　To sacrifice inspired,
Her merchants swore no goods to buy,
No boat to sail, no trade to ply,
　Nor aught a stamp required.

Said Isaac Sears, their leader,
　"A human lord, to shine,
His gloss from those about must take.
A rival stripped alone can make
　Mere decency divine.

" To gild the edge of title,
　For this is England made
Our sole resort for all we buy ;
For this they check the mills we ply.
　For this, our foreign trade.

"The noble class above us
　Who hold for gold the seive
Ours oozes through, would not eschew
Their royal rule — to others do
　What makes them humbly live.

" And shall we not live humbly
    Who only pride restrain?
  And buy at home more homely goods?"—
" Buy homespun !" rang from bay to woods.
    Then rang the looms amain.

  But keen and crafty tories,
    They prowled around at night ;
  They listened long and bought and sold
  And pried and plied, and some cajoled
    This homespun league to slight.

" Till stamps shall come from England
    We dare not wait," said Edes.
" If once a few our tories own,
    The wrong through all the land is sown :
    No hand the danger weeds."

" Resign the trust !" cried Boston,
    Her stamp-man's trade to stay.
  The cry, like thunder, threatened storm.
  Wild torches flashed ; the air was warm ;
    The people had their way.

"Resign!" ere long the echo
   Through all the land had rolled.
The sovereign people's arm was bared.
Through all the land no agent dared
   A hated stamp to hold.

"Our governors," howled the tories,
   "Shall sell to spell the crown."
The governors swore the task to take;
But we, we swore, our lives the stake,
   To put their purpose down.

The night before the Stamp Act
   Should take effect, ah me!
We slept not much; we melted lead;
We whetted steel; we planned ahead,
   We Sons of Liberty.

Then, when the morn was breaking,
   From seashore back to plain,
In all the towns were tolled the bells
That all began with doleful knells,
   As though for Freedom slain.

Anon, they rang out madly
  What might appear to be
The land's alarm-bell — nay not now ;
They pealed to hail the birth and vow
  Of Sons of Liberty.

New York sprang wild to hear them.
  Was flooded every way.
The people left their shops and mills.
The farmers flocked from all the hills ;
  The sailors from the. bay.

Now who would buy stamped papers ?
  The governor stood, agaze.
The stores before were all shut to ;
Enough of wiser work to do
  On this, a day of days !

"We would not, and we will not,"
  Said Isaac Sears, "submit."
The governor cried, "Your drums may beat,
But here a fort and there a fleet
  They scarcely thus outwit."

"The stamps," said James, his major,
      "A sword should cram them down
These choking throats, and him that squirms
The army crush as crush they worms —
      Or burn them out the town."

"Aha," replied our leader,
      "For this you soldiers came?
For this a wily governor
Sent word abroad the French made war?
      Aha, were we the game?

"Not daring yet to tax us,
      'For this a lawless crown
Bade British troopers take from hence
Free meals at every town's expense —
      Your pay to keep us down?

"For this to you from England
      Must our 'civilians' yield? —
You Braddock-men who boast but run
While ours stay back with Washington
      Alone to hold the field!

"Yes, yes, in genuine danger
　　We know who win the day ;
　Whose treasure here and blood it is
　That, from our fathers' time to this,
　　Have held each foe at bay.

"And need we now your army ?
　　You know — your sovereign too,
　Our wars are his that cross the sea,
　Or fret the Frenchmen here that he
　　Excuse may find for you.

"How strong, think you, our patience ?
　　How long before it tire ? —
　Ah, Britain's lion's whelp may get
　So tough by cuffs like this, as yet
　　To turn and rend its sire ! "

"Clear treason ! " cried the major ;
　　And "treason ! " cried his chief.
　The other's eye their fury brooked,
　Then calmly toward his comrades looked
　　To give his thoughts relief.

"There live such royal spirits,
   Their loyalty so great,
That when to wrong their ruler strays
The notion of the nation sways,
   The spirit of the state."

And then he told those courtiers
   Their words should he report.
They heard the people's groans that rose
To greet the words he bore, and chose
   To seek, near by, the fort.

The fort, the crowd surrounded.
   Its guns were at them swung.
"Now dare to fire you on the town,"
   The crowd cried out, "the gates go down,
   The governor find you hung."

The governor urged his honor;
   "Had pledged," he said, "his oath,
And ought to further Britain's aims." —
We thought New York had equal claims
   On oath and honor both.

"And let his pledge be given
    He let the stamps alone,"
Said Isaac Sears ; and all the crowd
Who heard him say it, shouted loud
    To make the words their own.

All day, with waning patience,
    That pledge was waited for ;
But, when there came an answer none,
No man could check a course begun
    To force the governor.

At night, the boys with torches,
    They started out for sport.
The house of James they sacked, and took
The army's flags his fear forsook,
    And marched them round the fort.

The governor owned his coaches,
    His sleighs, and horses trained.
They burst the barn before his eyes,
And dragged away with heartless cries
    The treasure there contained.

They framed a devil's image,
  The governor's image too;
And, side by side, made both careen,
Wheeled round and round the Bowling Green
  Where fort and fleet could view.

At last, of sleighs and coaches
  They formed a funeral pyre;
And, full in face of all the town,
Who only roared its roar to drown,
  They set the whole on fire.

Then came a wake and wailing,
  As ashes covered all;
And not a clause in laws unjust
The governor hoped on us to thrust
  But some one dared recall.

" A foe to all of England ! "
  " A foe to all of us ! "
" In Scotland went with Jacobites ! "
" Has vowed to murder here our rights ! —
  Ere that we toast him thus ! "

Then met the colony's council
　To vote what questioned none : —
"Those stamps Great Britain's crown assigned
　To agents here who all resigned ;
　None made the governor one."

At last the governor wavered ;
　He wrote an answer thus : —
"I wait the dawn of further light."
　Cried Isaac Sears, "the fox is bright.
　Morn makes him free from us.

"Now send we back this message : —
　'Awhile the town will wait
But four and twenty hours from now
Will hold the stamps or else will vow
　To hold no more debate.'"

The governor begged the army ;
　The army begged the fleet,
But no one cared to free the fort
Of papers borne to brave the sport
　Of those who filled the street.

The courage there of courtiers,
  It bowed to wisdom higher :
The power of right that ruled the mass,
It overawed the royal class ;
  They did not dare to fire.

They did not dare to kindle
  The flames of war, to fling
No light of glory round a throne
Where British freemen flushed alone
  To blush for Britain's King.

So nought was left the loyal
  Except to yield us all.
Our mayor took the stamps resigned,
And bore away to store behind
  The bolts of City Hall.

And, all relieved, the people,
  They cheered that right was done ;
Cried " Liberty and Property !
No stamps to curse the Colony ! "
  And parted, one by one.

At morning, all the papers
  Were published stamps without.
Men trusted not to notes but men.
The boats in harbor sailed again ;
  Their foes were moored in doubt.

And none a stamp had purchased,
  Or sealed himself a slave ;
And half of England, trust my word,
Were thrilled with joy, when proud they heard
  How we ourselves could save.

At last there came a daybreak
  When all the thankful kneeled ;
And bells were rung, and banners hung ;
And England's weal was drunk and sung, —
  The Stamp Act stood repealed.

Great Britain's lords in council
  Had talked of fire and ball ;
But, when they touched their liberties,
Met manhood in the colonies
  They could not thus inthrall.

THE LAST CRUISE OF THE GASPEE.

1772.

ONE windy day in March,
A ghost that brought dismay,
A vessel fleet, through snow and sleet,
Made Narraganset Bay.

There were smugglers in the bay,
And smugglers on the shore;
But loyal still to royal will
Ten times their number more.

But the captain railed at all,
His boasts afloat his ale;
"Rhode Island low is full, you know,
Of fellows fled from jail;

"And Puritans fled from law,
From kings they fear to fear.
Aha!" he laughed, "our loyal craft
Has brought the Cavalier!

"Our guns shall speak in tones
To make the whole bay ring;
And teach to each within their reach
To reverence here the King.

"Upon the sea are ships:
On bounties bound to fall,
Their sails we rip till flags they dip
To heed our royal call.

"Upon the shore are sheep;
Beside the sheep is wood:
Sure, fealty nice should sacrifice
To yield its navy food.

Some lawless were at sea;
Some lawless were on shore;
This ship, I ken, a band of men
Ten times as lawless bore.

The sheriff went and warned
The captain, angered sore,
By claims polite and chartered right,
To plunder there no more.

The captain waved his hand,
Said he, " The fleet has made
A vow devout to carry out
The English Acts of Trade."

Wrote Hopkins then from court,
"No warrant, none have you."
"The navy's crew injustice do,"
Wrote Governor Wanton too.

The captain dodged reply ;
"Let Boston urge his plea :
Not their affair ; the admiral there
His ship should oversee."

And then he turned away.
One heard him mutter near,
"The admiralty, I think I see,
Ship back their bounties here."

But yet the wronged ones wrote.
The admiral there was bold.
He swore to hang the Island gang,
And teach them who controlled.

And more, the man forgot,
An English soldier he,
To honor those the people chose
In a colony just and free.

" The navy know their trade,"
He rash to Wanton wrote ;
" In mere pretense and insolence
You board the Sovereign's boat."

Wrote Wanton, " Those at home,
Your lords, shall judge your note.
And every time it hint of crime,
Our sheriff boards the boat."

But months and months went on.
The cruiser fired away.
None plied an oar ; lived near the shore,
But feared to be its prey.

Cried Captain Lindsey bold,
  " An outrage none should bide !
Rhode Island grit must yet outwit,
  And trip the rascal's pride.

  " He knows my Packet here,
  Her trade, as well as I.
Now let him dare to sink me there,
  His guns shall I defy.

  " If down we go, the law,
  It floats to stand upon ;
If that go too, this case is through ;
  But Britain, more anon ! "

  So high his flag he flew ;
  And wide his sail he spread.
The cruiser fired ; her men perspired ;
  Her captain's face was red.

  " All hands aloft ! " he cried ;
  " All sail ! " and, while they strove,
Both ships, away in clouds of spray,
  Like squalls the waters clove.

When off of Nauquit Point,
Shrewd Lindsey knew his ground ;
Afar he steered, the bar he cleared,
And then the ship swung round.

Up tossed her canvas high ;
Then dipped, as round it ran,
A saucy way that seemed to say
Now catch me if you can.

The cruiser's captain saw ;
And mouthed an awful oath :
"Now catch I not, then fire and shot
Or bottom catch us both.

"Straight on, nor tack ! " he cried ;
" Straight on ! the bar is spare ;
The tide is high ; across we fly,
And head them off, up there."

Deep plowed the cruiser's prow
The broken waves below,
So bows a bull whose pride is full
To toss a stubborn foe.

She plunged and reeled and rolled.
Ah better had she tacked!
The sea, it flew the bulwark through.
The mainmast swayed and cracked.

The wind, it whistled there;
The boatswain whistled here.
The captain swore; the mainsail tore;
The jib had ripped its gear.

A flood had forced the deck.
The crew were floundering round.
Then, clean and chill, the whole was still;
The cruiser fast aground.

When Lindsey saw, such cheers
Went back from all his men,
The hostile crew, that heard them, flew
To man their guns again.

But Lindsey kept his course.
He here could do no more;
And, ere the night, the cruiser's plight
Had told along the shore.

"There stays the ship," said he,
"Till comes, anon, high tide."
"Till Providence shall lift her thence,"
John Brown, his friend, replied.

And Providence, at dusk,
Was rallied out to greet
Its Daniel Pearce who rattled fierce
His drum along the street.

"The cruiser lies aground!
High tide at three o'clock!
Who care to go and meet her so,
Come all to Fenner's dock!"

The people flocked, and lo,
In Captain Whipple's care,
Eight boats of Brown who roused the town
And sent the sailors there.

Each boat a captain steered;
And muffled every oar;
And, when they bent, the men who went,
All told, were sixty-four.

2

Their arms were culled with care
From all their friends could loan;
And all the yawls, for cannon balls,
Were stocked with paving-stone.

They battled wind and tide,
Three hours amid the gloom.
The midnight passed. They saw, at last,
The hated bulwarks loom.

"Who comes?" the watch called out.
"Who comes?" the captain cried.
Then swift alarmed, in tones that armed,
The crew that toward him hied.

"Move off!" the captain roared,
His pistol aiming well;
Then fired —— alack! fire answered back;
He started, staggered, fell.

Then, deathly dark and fierce
As tidal waves, where fleets
Are whelmed and whirled and downward
        hurled
Till the earthquake there retreats.

Our men, at Whipple's cry,
  "Up, up!" cleared every check;
And dashed and leapt and slashed and swept
  Across the cruiser's deck.

  Their men were all below;
  And ours on deck alone;
Clean work had done, nor fired a gun,
  The foe before them flown.

"Surrender here!" rang out;
  And out the 'cabin glanced
At first a few, then all the crew;
  Then one and all advanced.

  "First know," said Whipple then,
  "That here you sail no more;
And next prepare your boats to bear
  Yourselves and yours ashore."

  The sailors went and came,
  They came with bags and coats.
They called their roll, and said the whole
  They owned was in the boats.

Meantime, the captain's wound
The men who made had dressed;
And rowed him, sore but safe, ashore
With all his trunks possessed.

"All hands embark!" rang out;
And all the yawls were full;
Save one for those the work to close,
While off the rest should pull.

Three cheers anon bespoke
The vessel's farewell trip,
When, white as spray the former day,
Thin smoke made dim the ship.

Then seldom off her track
So fast had flown a crew,
While flashed the fire, and, streaming higher,
The red flag redder flew.

The cruiser sailed in state;
Once more her swivel plied;
Then powder, ball, and hull and all
The thunder's self defied.

High filled the heaven above.
Her ghost was not for heaven :
Each wounded cloud roared long and loud ;
Then back the whole was driven.

When all was still, there seemed
Faint sparks to fill the place —
"Nay, nay," said one, "the morning sun ;
A new day dawns apace ! "

It dawned for these, at least ;
When soon there hove in sight
Full half the town who crowded down
To cheer their deed that night.

But list ! the cheers were checked.
"Keep mum ! " the murmur spread ;
The government sought those who went,
A price on every head.

"Five hundred dollars down,
For him who tells of one,"
Was first proclaimed : but no one named
A man who aught had done.

"Five thousand," offered then,
  "To know who took the lead;
And half as much to know of such
  As joined him in the deed."

The King's commission, last,
  Sat half a year or more;
But not a word they ever heard
  Of all the sixty-four.

Forgotten were they then?
  They might have passed, by day,
Without a wink to make you think,
  Or hint that it was they.

But, when the night had come;
  When every door was locked;
The shutters fast, and blew the blast
  Till all the chimney rocked;

When, safe from eyes and ears,
  In homes where all were true,
The way those men were feasted then
  A king, full well, might rue.

And when the board was bare ;
When, round the roaring fire,
The nuts were cracked, and cider smacked
Till tooth and tongue would tire ;

When each his tale would tell
About that ship and night,
And still the way he dodged to-day
The British spy and spite ;

The boys that husked the corn
Would bend, anon to spring
And draw the ears, like swords, with cheers
To make the rafters ring !

The host who stirred the fire
Would stab till cinders flew !
You well had thought the flames he brought
The cruiser's would outdo !

The girls, where dashed the blaze
Like spray a ship concealed
Along the walls, would aim like balls
The apples red they peeled !

"To arms!" would cry the men;
    Then spry their prey purloin;
While mother's yarn would snap to darn
    The dance that all would join.

Ah, so we hushed the tale!
    Yet spies that sly would roam
Could not decoy the smallest boy
    To tell what passed at home.

We hushed the tale, yes, yes,
    Till proof made all believe
That all with nerve the weak to serve
    Applause from all receive.

We hushed it, till the hush
    Became our countersign
To save from those we knew were foes,
    And make our men combine.

We hushed it, till we learned
    What thousands would be free,
And longed to know which way to go
    To gain their liberty.

We hushed it, till we heard
The guns at Lexington ;
Then shouted loud, a mighty crowd,
" Our heroes lead us on ! "

2*

THE LEBANON BOYS IN BOSTON.

THE TEA PARTY, DECEMBER 16, 1773.

"NEW trouble down in Boston,"
    Was told us half the year;
Yet every week the postman came
    With something new to hear.

"Alas," they wrote, "that freedom's right
    Should life so hale beget
That lords its envied strength should drain
    With sword and bayonet.
Like leeches, cling the frigates
    About our wasted port;
The wharves inflamed with soldiers;
    An open sore the fort.

A foreign Board of Customs,
  Our courts cannot restrain,
Like vultures, where a scent of death,
  Their living come to gain.
Of old, when all stood up for rights,
  The Stamp Act was repealed;
We stooped to thank the Sovereign then,
  He thinks we now will yield."

We read, and thought together
  That something must be done ;
And we the ones to do it,
  We boys of Lebanon.

The words of Samuel Adams
  We heard a neighbor quote : —
" They silence our assembly.
  A sword is on its throat.
Our charter made a target,
  Our judgment-seat a fort,
Our men they rob for rations ;
  Our boys they shoot for sport.
Our faith that their horizons burst
  And zeniths held not down,

They ring with Acts to Tolerate,
  And bring a crippling crown.
I care not what to others
  A loyal feeling brings ;
To me it still shall loyal be
  To serve the King of Kings."

We heard, and swore together
  That work must be begun ;
And we the ones to do it,
  We boys of Lebanon.

We signed a pledge of union.
  To all the land we wrote.
We went to meet the postman.
  We read the Boston note : —
"In union only is there strength ;
  And strength our only stay.
Alas that some divide us ;
  Alas that some give way.
All trade with Britain broke we off ;
  But now the weak agree ;
'Enough,' they say, 'if none will taste,
  If none will trade with tea.'

"Who lie in wait the weakness spy.
      They try to trap it thus : —
' East India's losing traders
      Shall tea bring free ' to us.
   As though their thriving did not heap
      Her lap with tribute gold,
' Let them,' cries England, ' take the tax ;
      Let them the duties hold.'

" Already bound for Boston,
      May tea be on the waves,
   A bait flung out to tempt us
      To touch, and then be slaves.
   And if the strong should falter,
      Nor snatch the bait away,
   What keeps the weak from craft that makes
      The whole land England's prey ?
   What keeps temptation from the men
      By habits old unnerved ?
   What principle restrain them
      Who reason never served ? —

" And yet, this plot to parry,
      If Boston men conspire,

Their town may prove an altar ;
  Their fortunes melt in fire.
The sacrifice is ready ;
  Yet first they wait reply,
To know they own a country
  To save, before they die."

We met, and swore together,
  If fighting must be done,
In Boston we would do it,
  We boys of Lebanon.

We started out at midnight.
  We got the Indian suits,
We kept for sport or safety
  When red men raised recruits.
We packed them all in knapsacks.
  The girls our kisses dealt ;
Flung guns on every shoulder,
  And tomahawks in belt.
We crept along the forest.
  We dropped the ledges down.
We scattered near to Boston.
  We met within the town.

We hunted out our cousins.
We told them why we came.
" Aha," said they, " we plot the same.
We join you in the game."

They showed us then, at morning,
The Tree of Liberty,
Where those who planned the Stamp Act
Were hung in effigy.
A pole was now beside it.
A flag it bore flew high.
The church bells all were ringing.
A crowd had gathered nigh.

"To see this tree, the agent
Of stamps," we heard, "resigned.
Here too East India's agents
Should learn the people's mind:—
'All tea that comes from England,
Untouched to England goes ;
Or brand we these, its consignees,
Our own, our country's foes.'"
The people cheered the purpose.
The resolution passed.

The crowd about went homeward.
  The sky was overcast.

The message reached the agents.
  No promise would they sign.
Again the town demanded one.
  Again did all decline.
Then Boston's grand Committee
  Of Correspondence, said
" We write to all the province ; "
  And fast the riders sped.

From every hill and valley
  Came back, as though one word,
What Samuel Adams read with pride
  Where all the people heard : —
" Without a voice dissenting,
  We swear by you to stand.
Our wealth or life preventing,
  The tea shall never land."

Then dawned the stirring Sunday
  When swift the news was passed,
One tea-ship off the harbor ! " —
  The crisis came, at last.

Not many went to church then ;
  But all began to pray,
With eyes to duty open wide —
  The Puritanic way.

In haste we met together,
  Our work must be begun.
We planned how best to do it,
  We boys of Lebanon.
With Proctor named as captain,
  We formed, as soldiers free,
To cling like air and water there
  About the ship with tea.

The Town's Select Men waited on
  The vessel's consignees ;
But these the fort had waited on,
  Well locked with British keys.
True courtiers, they would tender
  The governor there their tea.
The governor called his councillors,
  The council said, "Not we ;
Our homes are with the people ;
  And we are not the ones

To hold the cup that Freedom drugs
  To them, ourselves, or sons."

The consignees still waited there
  While they the tea controlled;
The ship, in form, once entered,
  The harbor's laws must hold.
So quick the Town's Committee,
  With close at hand a writ,
They sealed the vessel's owner's word
  Not yet to enter it.

At Fanueil Hall, next morning,
  To answer bells that rung,
Men swarmed, like bees, to buzz before,
  Prepared to die, they stung.
The governor's sheriff waved his staff: —
  "You meet unlawfully!"
The staff but made them busier buzz,
  With Saxon loyalty.
The consignees they summoned.
  "The tea," these wrote, "we stack."
"The tea you ship to England,"
  The people answered back.

And then to ports in England,
　And all at home they wrote : —
"Tea taxers here, or traders,
　Our country's foes we vote.
Think not our men will waver,
　Our wives their vows abate ;
If bitter keep the herb they steep,
　More bitter still their hate."

Two tea ships more had anchored.
　Our guards, like nerves, were strung
From bay to every belfry's rope,
　The slightest stir had sprung.

Then spake the vessels' owners : —
　"Our cargoes, entered not,
In twenty days, the law will take ;
　The fleet their fate allot."
"Ere that you sail from Boston,"
　The Town's Committee said.
"Nay, nay, ere that," was answered back,
　"In Boston blood were shed."
They pointed down the harbor.
　Behold, the fleet below,

Like prongs along the channel,
　To rake a coming foe !
They pointed toward the castle.
　The flash of every gun
Bespoke an aim to pierce with flame
　A prey that dared to run !

No hope for writs of clearance,
　No hope in flight, they showed.
Thus checked, the people's purpose rose
　To bounds that overflowed.
Collector and comptroller,
　With solemn pleas they sought ;
The governor then, exulting
　To think his trap had caught.
" You mark the fleet and castle,
　Should trouble brew," said he,
" Your Hancocks, Rowes, and Phillips
　Might risk as much as we."

But Molineux said only,
　" They more would risk if slaves ;
Then, what were treasured most, would be
　Enough to give them graves."

"Of slaves," the governor answered,
　And glowed about the phrase ;
"Of slaves because a land has laws !"
　And passed the laws to praise ;
"And you would dare to break them? —
　And reason, what of it? —
I trust in human nature,
　When reason says, submit."

"We trust in human nature,"
　Said Young, who near him stood ;
"And peace, where thrives oppression,
　It does not deem a good.
We trust in human nature ;
　The conscience, governing there,
The right may guard as well as kings
　With crowns their dearest care.
Love rules in human nature,
　For, all of history through,
The slaves have been the many,
　The tyrants been the few."

The governor turned in anger ;
　"Well, well, we then shall see.

Your hint of flint can frighten
   No clearance here from me."

Still met the town together,
   Their final vote to take..
Not one, of seven thousand there,
   Had wish the peace to break.
Said Quincy, "Crowds and shoutings
   Not now can end the strife.
Come other crowds, and other shouts ;
   And go estate and life.
The structures fair of freedom
   Men rear beneath the sky,
Press down on deep foundations,
   Where thousands buried lie.
Our course we well may ponder :
   A bow may span the cloud,
But hope's first march beneath the arch
   Meet flash and bolt and shroud."
The people paused and pondered ;
   But, when they called for hands,
Not one of all but voted,
   The tea, it never lands.

And then we met together;
  If fighting must be done,
Our time had come to do it,
  We boys of Lebanon.
Another morn the vessels
  The fleet and fort would hold;
Then, who could say what power could stay
  The tea from being sold.

Close by we sought our quarters.
  We cleared our knapsacks quick.
We donned our Indian guises.
  We stained our cheeks with brick.
Anon, we all were ready;
  Half, tomahawks in hand;
And half, with muskets only,
  We heard our last command.

A moment then we waited.
  We knew the danger there.
We looked above for courage.
  We bent below in prayer.
We swore by God in Heaven,
  Our names to keep from all.

We swore to stand together,
  Till death should doom to fall.
We swore, by truth and honor,
  Should half essay to flee,
To cast that half the harbor in
  To perish with the tea.

The twilight long had tarried.
  The darkness deeper grew.
In old South Church, the people
  Still pondered what to do.
The dimness vailed our coming.
  We listened near the door,
Till Adams said, "For freedom fled,
  We here can do no more."
And then we yelled together,
  "To Griffin's wharf come on!"
All ready we to do the rest,
  We boys of Lebanon.

Then off flew some as sentries
  To stand and sound alarms,
Should coming spies or soldiers
  Compel resort to arms.

The twilight long had tarried.
The darkness deeper grew ;
"Full time," said we, "to take our tea!"
The people thought so too.

To Griffin's wharf we led them.
We rowed, and reached the ships.
No captain there, nor sailor,
Dared open once his lips.
We crowded every gangway.
We brought out every chest ;
Tore every wrap to guard the tea,
And steeped the bay our best.
No time was there for shouting,
No wish was there for strife.
Three hours we wrought in silence,
Each thankful more for life.
Anon, the work was ended ;
Anon, we back could row,
The heaven was black above us ;
The harbor black below.

None thought on shore to cheer us,
Though all had waited there.

3

Their silence seemed the silence,
  Where souls have flown to prayer.
Their silence seemed the silence
  Of war's reserves, where breath
Is hushed to hear the order,
  To call, they fear, to death.
Their silence seemed the silence
  Of ˌheavens, close and warm,
Ere, like a shell that houses hell,
  They burst to free the storm.

As hushed as on a Sabbath,
  The people homeward went ;
Their eyes alone transparent
  To show the soul's content.
But we, we met together,
  When all the work was done,
To toast the dawn of freedom,
  We boys of Lebanon.

Then, early stirred at morning,
  We left with Paul Revere,
Who through the South went riding off
  To bear, from Boston, cheer.

We spread through all the country.
　We told, how all was done ;
Till all the shoremen stored away
　A tomahawk and gun.
Throughout the land, no tory
　Would brave their sworn attack.
East India found no agent.
　The tea that came went back.

But, better far for freedom,
　There · flew, from mouth to mouth,
From soul to soul, a tide to roll,
　And sweep from North to South.
The source was patriotic ;
　It flowed to flood the land.
No colony held its borders ;
　No jealousy could withstand.
Before, men talked of union ;
　But now was union won,
When all the land, on every hand,
　Held boys of Lebanon.

THE CROWN'S FIGHT AGAINST THE TOWN'S RIGHT.

"A GALLOPING horse is coming
    Across the field ! — do you mark ? " —
We woke and flew to the window.
    We peered away in the dark.

The night, a cloud about us,
    It bore a bolt to fear.
What flashed and clashed ? — who brought it ? —
    " I, I ! " cried Paul Revere.

" The British are off for Concord
    To seize the colony's arms !
And Dawes and I the river
    Stole over, and over the farms."

" But wait you, Paul, a moment;
    A guide shall ride below.
Below you cross the forest;
    Nor plain the way to know. "

" Quick, quick ! " cried Paul, " about us
    Shine eyes, like owls at night.
Like stars that bar the darkness,
    The whole to cage in light."

Yet wait you, Paul, and waiting
    How, say, does Boston fare ? " —
" Alas," he sighed, " no saying
    How many shall breakfast there.

" Ever since the Port Bill lowered
    The flags of all its fleet,
The town had starved, if others
    Had spared it nothing to eat.

" Are strung their forts to fasten
    A chain about Boston Neck;
Is strung the bay with frigates,
    All trade to dog and check.

"Like fate shall doom the city
    Till all yield up, they say,
  Free meetings, courts, and charters,
    All rights they wrest away.

"And yield that all the ardent
    Who dare the truth to tell,
  They bear away to Britain;
    They find a felon's cell.

"And those who called our Congress,
    They swear to take to-day. —
  High time to rouse the country!
    High time to save the prey!"

"Off, off!" we cried, and parted.
    Then dragged from under the hay
  The guns, manure had mantled
    When borne from Boston Bay.

  Our wives poured out the powder
    From pockets and tucks they ripped;
  And cartridges too, from Boston
    In candle boxes shipped.

With God we left the women ;
   The hill had hardly won,
When wild the bell rang telling
   Of Paul in Lexington.

At midnight, saw he Charlestown.
   Not two had struck the clock :
That trembling church and belfry,
   Had rallied all its flock.

They sought the green together ;
   Set guards on every road ;
Then sought the inn to measure
   The fate they might forbode.

Ten times their band in number
   Were foes they watched before ;
And here should they withstand them,
   Or fly to join with more.

" Stand here ! " said Jonas Parker ;
   " The law, it armed the town."
" And here," said Clark, their pastor,
   " Be right and shame the crown.

" What though their guns, in thunder,
    Arouse a rain of blood? —
Their echoes yet may yonder
    Proclaim how comes the flood.

" If crowd there then to Concord
    The men to save the stores,
Our limbs, though red and falling,
    Were ripe to all their cores.

" Are times of war, when cannon
    Are clogged by only rills;
Our blood may check the Briton,
    More check the more he spills.

" Are times that twigs, though buried,
    Have snared an avalanche so;
How blest our lives if ended
    Where tyranny shared our woe.

" We are few; yet view a witness, —
    The church, from Heaven on high, —
How right may move to triumph
    With only one — to die!"

He paused — the door flew open.
 All heard a watch call out : —
" Full drive a horseman coming !
 May come an English scout ! "

And out they flew to face him ;
 But not too quick to meet
No enemy, only a neighbor,
 There galloping up the street.

" The foe are come ! " he stammered ;
 " They capture all they meet.
I dodged a man and musket.
 And hark ! — you hear their feet ! "

We hearkened ; and heard, behind him,
 A tramp that well might scare ;
It crushed the brain of moisture ;
 It clotted the lungs with air.

It chilled the heart that shivered
 A load of fear to bear ;
Till duty sprang indignant
 To drum to courage there.

3*

"Sound drums and guns!" said Parker,
  "And bell! If these but halt,
Where time is all we plan for,
  We win though none assault."

They halted, then drew nearer. —
  What need of halting more? —
They came, of old an army;
  We never had fought before.

We stood but sixty farmers,
  Those homes and wives between,
Whose hands, up waved or wringing,
  Seemed fringing all that green.

"Be theirs the blame!" said Parker,
  "Fire not, till fire is sent.
Stand firm; God's House behind us,
  And Heaven when balls are spent."

Athwart the gray of morning,
  None knew how large a force
Came crowding across the common,
  With cries and orders hoarse.

At double quick, and onward,
　With bayonets fixed, they came ;
Deep, wide and wild about us,
　As red they burst as flame.

Before them rode their leader,
　Our steadfast front to curse.
" Lay down those arms ! " he shouted,
　" You villains, all disperse ! "

But, true to law and country,
　Scarce one his musket dropped.
The foe before us faltered,
　Broke up, moved slower, stopped.

" You rebels ! " roared the leader,
　While up his pistol came ;
A hint his minions welcomed ;
　We saw them all take aim.

We saw, but all had waited,
　When " Fire ! " their leader cried ;
And shot, and howled, " Surround them ! "
　And round us spurred to ride.

A flash ! — alas the lawless ! —
   Up surged the fiery flood ;
All overwhelmed, our brothers
   Were sinking, drenched with blood.

" Serve right before the Briton ! "
   Cried Parker's soul that sped ;
And scores, it seemed, were wounded ;
   And half we feared were dead.

" Away ! " a voice repeated,
   " Away while yet you may.
To stay were now but murder !
   To wall and fence away ! "

Off sped we then to pick them,
   Like Indians, one by one,
But walls, in smoke between us,
   The foe were wise to shun.

They cheered and left for Concord.
   Our wounded home we bore ;
And then we vowed, in Concord
   To meet the foe once more.

THE RALLY OF THE FARMERS.

CONCORD, APRIL 19, 1775.

THE Concord men had warning.
  They all, through half the night,
Like ants along the meadows,
  Had dragged the stores from sight.

And, days before the march came,
  Our Salem Congress too,
They knew the arms were menaced,
  And here had left but few.

And here flew men till morning
  Rolled up, with tides of light,
A surf of bayonets, flashing,
  To drive the town to flight,

Then sought they heights that Heaven
   Made bright, and not the foe ;
Whence breezes borne were sweeter
   Than war notes blown below.

There farmers, roused in Bedford,
   In Littleton and Carlisle,
In Westford, Lincoln, Chelmsford,
   Flocked in, through each defile.

And there, when came a rumor
   How Lexington men had fared,
No lion loose a vengeance
   More bold then theirs had dared.

Anon, they watched the Briton
   About their village rave,
Of flour full sixty barrels
   · Tear open, stave from stave.

They saw him spike their cannon,
   Pave all their pond with balls,
And wheels pile up and wagons
   To block the ways like walls.

They saw a foe that feared it
   Their liberty-pole cut down ;
Then burn with all the pile there
   That yet might burn the town.

The flames had caught the court-house.
   Our men were hard to stay.
But " Justice, " cried our leader,
   " Will house in Heaven to-day.

"We wait, till here divided
   They drift, our arms to take ;
Or flood, like waves, their columns ;
   Where waits this ridge, they break ! "

Just then, by both the bridges
   The foe a force had placed ;
A check to ours beyond them,
   While further stores they traced ;

A check to men who viewed it,
   While maids and mothers turned
To fly from houses plundered,
   When sacked, it might be, burned.

"The north bridge," argued Hosmer;
   "On, on, keep back the foe!"
"No man of mine from Acton,"
   Said Davis, "fears to go."

And then our leader Barrett
   The word to follow gave,
Where moved the men of Acton
   Behind their captain brave.

With arms beside them trailing,
   In double file and slow,
Naught flaunted but undaunted,
   These farmers faced their foe.

The British rushed to ruin
   The bridge, and then retire.
"Let stay!" cried Major Buttrick.
   They answered but to fire. .

Dead Davis fell, and Hosmer.
   "For God's sake," Buttrick cried,
"Fire, fire!" — and three fell dying
   Upon the British side.

Thus Heaven, where hung the impulse
  A grander man to mould,
Had Saxon hurled on Saxon,
  The new world on the old.

The British swift retreated.
  Their colonel, where they sped,
First marched to reinforce them ;
  Then all for Boston led.

But now were men from Reading
  And Sudbury marshaled out,
And Woburn, wild to flank them :
  Their march became a rout.

We had but half their number ;
  But made so dangerous,
Those Red-coats journeyed safer
  With Spanish bulls than us.

With guards at every turning,
  They covered well their flanks ;
But smoke that leapt from ambush
  Shot, ghost-like, through their ranks.

From Dedham, Essex, Danvers,
　　From Chelsea, Marblehead,
From Dorchester, from Brookline,
　　Our men to trap them sped.

Back slunk their line before us,
　　A weary, wounded snake :
Up hill, down dale, round river,
　　It dragged, with bleeding wake.

The whole reserve in Boston
　　Poured out to help them back ;
But all the trees and houses
　　Seemed haunting now their track.

They turned to shoot our mothers ;
　　They turned our babes to kill ;
Our vengeance raged at Cambridge,
　　And reigned at Prospect Hill.

Down sweeping, Heath and Warren
　　A charge to break them led ;
Then Pickering's men from Salem
　　Burst, storm-like o'er their head.

Full night had known its fullest,
  Ere all their fears were stilled ;
Full nine score badly wounded,
  And more than threescore killed.

Nor, till they touched the river,
  Beyond the fleet had passed,
Our eyes that watched the danger
  Were once behind us cast.

And then, alas to view it !
  Hot, bitter tears we shed ;
Full thirty found we wounded,
  And well nigh sixty dead.

Our wives had lost their husbands ;
  Our mothers lost their boys ;
The sun in blood that evening,
  Had set on all their joys.

Yet, when we clasped those corpses,
  As over Huns of old,
It seemed the skies were filling
  With souls for ours enrolled.

Our prayers when all were buried,
  Were vows to Heaven that led,
From hearts that hailed the glory
  Of passing toward their dead.

With that we held our weapons ;
  Had foiled the British aims ;
We held our homes : — the women
  Had quenched the Court-house flames.

Our men had fought the army ;
  Were soldiers made the hour
The crude, provincial farmer
  Had proved and knew his power.

And so, despite the anguish
  That filled the morrow's morn,
The voice that wept betokened
  A nation, newly born.

"And I," said Samuel Adams,
  "Thank God this day to see ! "
"And I," came back from Hancock,
  " It makes the new world free ! "

ETHAN ALLEN.

TICONDEROGA, MAY 10, 1775.

WHEN rang the bell at Lexington
　Our men had flown to arms ;
And women now, for miles around,
　Were all who ploughed the farms.

All Boston seemed, where Red-coats shrank,
　A foiled and wounded prey ;
Yet one, fresh draughts of blood drank in
　From fleets that filled the bay.

And soon, like words men breathe at night
　Near foes who plot their death,
The whisper wild was urged along
　Our pale wives' haunted breath.

That, while like mighty mushrooms grew
　　Their earthworks night by night,
By day our threatened men could find
　　No arms with which to fight.

The story awed Connecticut,
　　And our Assembly there ;
And Mott and Phelps arose and swore
　　To make the want their care.

They passed to Pittsfield ; there were joined
　　By Easton, Brown, and more ;
Then on to Bennington, and there
　　Could muster full two score.

A feeble force to brave a fort
　　Where each yard yawned a gun ;
Yet those who slight the light of stars
　　But seldom see their sun.

The sun that dawned before them here,
　　That doubt could scarce survive,
Was Ethan Allen's sword that flashed
　　To make Vermont alive.

As thick as rills that rift in Spring
  Each bond the sun destroys,
Came pouring over all those hills
  His grand Green Mountain Boys,

Two hundred hardy men, as brave
  As ever mountains reared,
Fought famine, frost, and bears at home,
  And naught beyond it feared.

Ere long, a shout the vale rang out;
  Then "Onward!" called the voice
Of Allen, named to lead the lines,
  Who all had hailed the choice.

But one who heard his charger spurred,
  And cried, as came he near,
"Nay, nay, in me your leader see,
  For Cambridge sent me here."

"And Cambridge, Cambridge, what has she,"
  Cried Mott and Phelps, "to say?
Our Hartford sent us forth, and we
  Bade Allen lead the way."

"And we," cried those Vermonters true,
  " We came with Allen here :
And all agree none brave as he
  To lead the mountaineer."

The other hushed to hear them cry ;
  And honor high to all :
They faced the traitor Arnold thus,
  Who thus began his fall.

And honor due to Allen too ;
  ' High compliment, I trow ! —
Where good and guile were joined awhile
  The former found a foe.

Three days they tramped, then Allen spake
  " We split in parties three ;
One north, one south, one onward straight
  To seek the lake with me.

"From north and south, our comrades fleet,
  They forward all that floats,
To make for Shoreham where we wait
  To cross when come the boats.

" Now fall in line, and follow close
   Behind the lantern's glare,
Beyond, Ticonderoga dawns ;
   At morn, we breakfast there."

Then, down the hunter's trail, our line
   Wound on as glides a snake,
Then, late at night, prepared to spring
   Lay coiled beside the lake.

" Now off," said Allen, " North and South,
   And list for sound of oar,"
Alas, to think that Heaven above
   Should favor man no more !

To north and south we scattered far,
   We listened o'er and o'er,
But not a sound, to north or south,
   The empty breezes bore.

A few could find the boats to cross,
   Alas, but all too few !
Night sped, and Allen, near the fort
   Could count but eighty-two.

4

"My men," he muttered, "look — the light, —
　　Before can cross the lake
　One boat again for other men,
　　The morning full shall break.

"Yet note the wall. — You know it well, —
　　Ten times our force, if seen,
　Though clad in mail, could never scale
　　Those cannon thick between.

" And here the boats. — What say you all?
　　Your guns lift up, no breath.
　The lake cross here? — or weapons there?
　　Face cowardice? — or death?

" Your guns all up? your hearts all true?
　　How well! Had one turned back,
　Yon mountains heaped not rocks enough
　　To hide his skulking track.

"He easier might have faced, at home,
　　Where snow-capped hills all flame,
　The sun! than wives and little ones
　　Whose cheeks were fired with shame.

" How oft, without a roof for these,
   Your grants of land all spurned,
With no more gold to buy when sold
   The homes you once had earned ;

" How oft, when all was torn from you,
   And all had urged in vain
Your chartered rights, the common law,
   And all that God makes plain ;

" How oft then have you prayed aloud
   That Heaven would send you down
A chance from off your country's brow
   To hurl the hated crown !

" That chance has come ! But once for all
   Can dawn a day like this.
And all the glory meant for life
   Keeps midnight if one miss ;

" But if he win — ah yonder sun
   Sheds not a splendor fit
With which to rise above his name
   Or earth that welcomes it !

" Yes earth! For they forgot, our lords,
     They dealt with Puritans,
  True sons of those whom Cromwell led,
     Whose right means every man's ;

" Who take their individual ills
     For proofs of general pain ;
  And where one prince has made them wince
     Strike all, that man may reign.

" And they forgot, we mountaineers,
     High rangers like the Swiss,
  Had learned to value freedom's world
     By looking down on this !

" And longed to prove it ! Aye, my men,
     To-day you show with me
  How freemen, forced for self to care,
     Crown self, and keep it free

" Now quick, but quiet — Start with steel.
     Nor fire till sure you hit.
  First through the gate, if through we may.
     If not, then over it.

" I lead. You follow. Should I fall,
　　Move on, my corpse may give
　At least a vantage ground ! Move up.
　　The cause, it is, must live ! "

Then Allen left, and leapt behind
　　First Arnold, rivaling still ;
Then Brown and Easton, all the line
　　Stole softly up the hill.

The startled sentry aimed his gun
　　Straight out at Allen's face ;
But Allen flew, as flashed the flint,
　　To dash it from its place.

The sentry dodged, and darted down
　　A passage through the mound.
In poured our men ; you might have thought
　　The sentry had been drowned.

Swift, one by one, by Allen led,
　　They plunged along the gloom ; ,
No thought of scores that, just beyond,
　　Might make the place their tomb.

On ran the sentry; on our men, —
  Their mountains gave no game,
Nor guide so swift to apprehend
  The grounds on which they came.

At last, uploomed in dusky light,
  Close choking all the way,
One armed with ball and bayonet
  To hold the whole at bay.

"Take heed!" he cried. "We take it, man,"
  Went back where Allen sped;
Then clashed his sword that glanced the gun
  To cleave the crouching head.

"Have mercy," groaned the wounded wretch.
  Cried Allen, "Down your gun!
Hist, hist, my men, within the fort!
  And now the barrack, run!"

No need to bid. A moment more,
  Our boys had crowned their race;
And closed, with shouts like thousands, round
  The soldiers' sleeping place.

Meantime, "The captain!" Allen cried ;
  And scarce the word had said,
Ere on a door was pounding loud
  To rouse his foe from bed.

It opened partly, where behold!
  In robes as white as fleece,
The chief, beside his blushing bride,
  A picture stood of peace.

"Surrender!" ordered Allen then,
  "If not, by Him on high,
Your garrison, my men beset —
  Nor hope for quarter, — die!"

The captain's anger now had burst
  The spell of night's repose.
"Surrender!" hissed he — then turned pale
  To hear those shouts that rose —

"And what, I beg to know, and who
  Are all your rebel crew?
And whose the name in which you come
  And bid to yield to you?"

"Of God Jehovah?" Allen cried,
    " And " — while his sword flashed high —
"The Continental Congress, man ! "
    And now had flashed his eye.

    It flashed to vent the conscious force
      Of him who fights for man,
    The power that burns to sweep from earth
      Each prince or partisan.

    And Congress then, as Congress aye,
      The child of God to shield —
    Jehovah in the man at least —
      It forced the foe to yield.

    The day was won; the garrison
      Filed out across the green.
    More general welcome where they came,
      I ween was seldom seen.

    Not one who bore a cumbering gun
      Or lugged a lazy sword,
    But some one, all politely bent,
      To lend his aid implored.

Alack, we stacked our shoulders full,
  Relieved of all their care ;
Then, Arab-like, good will we proved
  By taking breakfast there.

For days we never turned aside
  Our gazes amorous,
Till, like a bride to watch with pride,
  Went each one home with us.

And then the fort — ah me, to see
  The trouble rare it took
To clear the space, and give the place
  A less unfriendly look !

Ten score of cannon, hills of flint,
  And tons of guns and balls —
We waited weeks, to find the means
  To cart them out the walls.

But first, we mailed a message home ;
  And I have heard it said,
When Congress heard, the floor was wet
  With tears those men had shed.

  4 *

At Cambridge, at the news, the air
  With such a shout was rent,
It almost equaled there the roar
  Of guns our fort had sent.

And Allen?—Allen lived and thrived,
  The chief of all that tract,
Where fleets and forts and all gave way
  When bold our boys attacked.

But war has tricks; and life has turns;
  Misfortunes find the true;
And Allen ónce, across the sea,
  Was borne a prisoner too.

Yet heroes' homes are human hearts.
  There, English crowds would cling
About the·form of him they felt
  Was grand, beyond their king.

He came back home and church bells rang —
  You might, in truth, have thought
A second Christmas day had come,
  And Saviour's advent brought!—

And guns were fired ; and, rank on rank,
  His State made haste to call
This bravest soul of all her sons,
  The General there of all.

And all the people while he lived,
  They loved that eagle eye ;
And when he died — ah friends, you know,
  Such spirits cannot die.

To-day, go search those mountains green,
  Those valleys, humbly trod
By souls whose simple faith is firm
  To country, home, and God ;

Ask men who own those towering trees,
  Or plant those hillocks steep,
The school boys, bounding back from school,
  Or watching well the sheep ;

The housewives, where in thrifty homes
  The generous meal is spread ;
The sisters, softly handing down
  The Book when prayers are said ;

Ask all, who value aught they own,
   Whose fame all value most?
The flushing cheek and flashing eye
   Will figure him they boast.

Nay more, to-day, in any State
   Our whole broad land throughout,
If aught to forward waits so weak
   No hand dare aid its doubt;

If fashion's forces bind the soul
   So conscience hardly breathes,
Where love is fettered, truth is hushed,
   And right her sabre sheathes;

If all the crowd below are cowed
   Because some power that reigns,
Each fortress holds that aids defense,
   And arm that each retains;

And yet, if dreams of braver life
   That always bless the true,
Rouse those whose foes swarm thick, at morn,
   As clouds to trembling dew;

Then would you fire these on, like powers
   That, lightning-shod, flash nigh,
And crush to storms each cloud that forms
   Where heaven would cleanse the sky : —

Wherever faith should conflict face,
   And wrong compliance shun ;
Just name the name of Allen there —
   The strife, you find, begun.

HOW BARTON TOOK THE GENERAL.

NARRAGANSETT BAY, JULY 10, 1777.

"THEIR wrongs are due to Prescott,"
  Brave William Barton said;
"He made them wear his colors there,
  Though blood should dye them red.

"Blame not the line ; the leader
  Has filled the town with fear.
No heel more base could Britain place
  To foul her footstool here!"

"Say footpath here," said Potter ;
  "Just now their doorsteps go
To pave the way where, once a day,
  His lordship walks, you know.

"Then meets he three together,
 Or one who wears his cap,
He 'Rebel!' calls; their heads are balls;
 His cane a club to rap."

"Small vengeance!" answered Barton;
 "Yet wrinkles show the will.
A grazing ass that kicks but grass
 Has tricks that yet may kill.

"The Friends lift hats to no one,
 Is that in them remiss?
Yet one in town his steed rode down,
 And he imprisoned for this.

"Then Trip — none knew the reason —
 One day to jail was sent.
Whereat, in grief that sought relief,
 His wife to see him went.

"She heard but, 'No; nor write him
 Till hangmen execute!' —
Who domineers o'er woman's tears
 Is less a man than brute!

" For one, with guns to follow
    And force a way, I swear
To trap the wretch, and hither fetch,
    Or die beside him there."

"Sure death, sure death!" was muttered.
    "The troops fill every road.
If one could fly then one could try,
    But where another mode?"

" He quarters yet," said Barton,
    "At Quaker Overton's.
The house you know; the land is low;
    The bay behind it runs.

"The fields are full of soldiers;
    No hope to reach him thus.
His fleet, they say, fill half the bay;
    Yet half that leaves for us.

"Three frigates guard his quarters.
    What then? — when clouds are hung
From starry heights to vail the lights
    Not there for evil swung;

" When rough are breeze and breakers,
Then soft, with muffled oar
And heaven to keep. I dare to creep
Between the fleet to shore."

His comrades hushed to heed him.
Then gave their hands and swore.
With heaven to keep, that they would creep
Between the fleet to shore.

The night was dark and lowry;
The bay was wild and wide;
Each patient oar they bent before
Like velvet stroked the tide.

Above, through English bulwarks.
Came sounds of English feet.
Above, " All 's well ! " rang out to tell
How full the hostile fleet.

They pulled to pass a guard-boat,
To land, pour out, divide;
To file about, the prey to scout
And trap on every side.

Each party prowled in danger ;
  Crept softly toward and round
A sentry near a guard-house here,
  And there a camping ground.

At last, the net was ready,
  Was held at every side,
Brave Barton sly the front door nigh
  Had found it open wide.

" Who comes ? " there called a sentry.
  " Your countersign ? " he asked.
" Have none to-night " — the tone was light —
  " Have here deserters passed ? "

" Ah, from the fleet ? " was answered.
  " Yes," Barton hissed, "from one ! "
And, quick as dashed a tiger lashed,
  . Had clutched his throat and gun.

The sentry cowed and gave it ;
  Lay gunless, gagged and bound.
Our men, at last, the door had passed,
  Nor yet had roused a sound.

The Quaker host sat reading.
 "For what come you?" he said;
Then, when he heard "For Prescott," stirred
 To point them overhead.

As soft as cats, the captors
 Stole up each tell-tale stair,
And crossed a floor, — was locked a door
 Nor time, nor sound to spare.

Then Sisson, one of thousands,
 A burly, patriot black,
Bent down; took aim with head and frame. —
 One butt — the door flew back!

The shock their prey had started.
 He sprang in haste from bed.
He clutched to hold his watch of gold
 That hung beside his head.

"And darkness take you robbers
 From sword," he cried, "and shot!" —
"No robber harms; put by those arms,"
 He heard, nor left the spot.

"You, general, stand a captive.
    And see — these daggers three.
  You breathe a word, you make us heard,
    That breath your last shall be.

"Move on!" — "I dress," said Prescott.
    But Barton bowed polite ;
"Nay, nay, not so ; we came, you know,
    Without our wives to-night.

"Your hands bear all you carry.
    Like pitch the night, and hot.
  Your last resort. — The time is short,
    Thank God you lie not shot."

Down stairs, they marched the captive,
    But hark ! — the neighboring room ! —
  A window crashed ! — Out Barton dashed,
    Peered anxious past the gloom.

All well ! — The noise was over ;
    Another captive bound ;
  The general's aid a prisoner made
    Just where his feet found ground.

Then general, aid, and sentry,
  A sword at every head,
Their captors wound the camp around,
  Like needles there and thread.

At last, they reached the water ;
  At last, were off to glide
With muffled oar between the shore
  And boats that watched beside.

Above, through English bulwarks,
  Came sounds of English feet.
Above, " All 's well " rang out to tell
  How fooled the hostile fleet.

Anon, their stroke was bolder :
  For Warwick Point they bore.
A coach and pair were there to bear
  Their captive far on shore.

Then Prescott broke the silence : —
  "The push was boldly planned."
Said Barton, " Yes, and with success ;"
  And took his reins in hand.

Success it was for Newport.
  The foe knew all it meant,
The prison door they closed no more
  To bar our innocent.

Success it was for Barton.
  In days like those of old
No envy rife, nor party strife,
  Would slur a deed so bold.

Through all the homes in Newport,
  Through all our camps afar,
His name was rung, his praise was sung,
  As victory's morning star.

Where dawned that day of freedom
  The man whose light so shone,
So blest his land, appeared more grand
  Because he rose alone.

Ere long, a grateful Congress
  Sent one that for him brought
A sword, with rare inscriptions there
  To treasure all they thought.

In green Vermont they gave him
  A generous grant of land ;
They felt this one enough had done
  On soil, his own, to stand.

But what of all was fittest,
  Was cheered in every tent,
Were words that raised the one we praised
  To lead our regiment.

Where weak and few the forces
  Our land could call its own,
We knew this man would hold the van
  And fight, though left alone.

www.ingramcontent.com/pod-product-compliance
Lightning Source LLC
Chambersburg PA
CBHW022148020726
47496CB00008B/2621